THE KNIGHTS OF ARTHUR

THE KNIGHTS OF ARTHUR

by Frederik Pohl

CONTENTS

I

There was three of us—I mean if you count Arthur. We split up to avoid attracting attention. Engdahl just came in over the big bridge, but I had Arthur with me so I had to come the long way around.

When I registered at the desk, I said I was from Chicago. You know how it is. If you say you're from Philadelphia, it's like saying you're from St. Louis or Detroit—I mean *nobody* lives in Philadelphia any more. Shows how things change. A couple years ago, Philadelphia was all the fashion. But not now, and I wanted to make a good impression.

I even tipped the bellboy a hundred and fifty dollars. I said: "Do me a favor. I've got my baggage booby-trapped—"

"Natch," he said, only mildly impressed by the bill and a half, even less impressed by me.

"I mean *really* booby-trapped. Not just a burglar alarm. Besides the alarm, there's a little surprise on a short fuse. So what I want you to do, if you hear the alarm go off, is come running. Right?"

"And get my head blown off?" He slammed my bags onto the floor. "Mister, you can take your damn money and—"

"Wait a minute, friend." I passed over another hundred. "Please? It's only a shaped charge. It won't hurt anything except anybody who messes around, see? But I don't want it to go off. So you come running when you hear the alarm and scare him away and—"

"No!" But he was less positive. I gave him two hundred more and he said grudgingly: "All right. If I hear it. Say, what's in there that's worth all that trouble?"

"Papers," I lied.

He leered. "Sure."

"No fooling, it's just personal stuff. Not worth a penny to anybody but me, understand? So don't get any ideas—"

He said in an injured tone: "Mister, naturally the *staff* won't bother your stuff. What kind of a hotel do you think this is?"

"Of course, of course," I said. But I knew he was lying, because I knew what kind of hotel it was. The staff was there only because being there gave them a chance to knock down more money than they could make any other way. What other kind of hotel was there?

Anyway, the way to keep the staff on my side was by bribery, and when he left I figured I had him at least temporarily bought. He promised to keep an eye on the room and he would be on duty for four more hours—which gave me plenty of time for my errands.

*

I made sure Arthur was plugged in and cleaned myself up. They had water running—New York's very good that way; they always have water running. It was even hot, or nearly hot. I let the shower splash over me for a while, because there was a lot of dust and dirt from the Bronx that I had to get off me. The way it looked, hardly anybody had been up that way since it happened.

I dried myself, got dressed and looked out the window. We were fairly high up—fifteenth floor. I could see the Hudson and the big bridge up north of us. There was a huge cloud of smoke coming from somewhere near the bridge on the other side of the river, but outside of that everything looked normal. You would have thought there were people in all those houses. Even the streets looked pretty good, until you noticed that hardly any of the cars were moving.

I opened the little bag and loaded my pockets with enough money to run my errands. At the door, I stopped and called over my shoulder to Arthur: "Don't worry if I'm gone an hour or so. I'll be back."

I didn't wait for an answer. That would have been pointless under the circumstances.

After Philadelphia, this place seemed to be bustling with activity. There were four or five people in the lobby and a couple of dozen more out in the street.

I tarried at the desk for several reasons. In the first place, I was expecting Vern Engdahl to try to contact me and I didn't want him messing with the luggage—not while Arthur might get nervous. So I told the desk clerk that in case anybody came inquiring for Mr. Schlaepfer, which was the name I was using—my real name being Sam Dunlap—he was to be told that on no account was he to go to my room but to wait in the lobby; and in any case I would be back in an hour.

"Sure," said the desk clerk, holding out his hand.

I crossed it with paper. "One other thing," I said. "I need to buy an electric typewriter and some other stuff. Where can I get them?"

"PX," he said promptly.

"PX?"

"What used to be Macy's," he explained. "You go out that door and turn right. It's only about a block. You'll see the sign."

"Thanks." That cost me a hundred more, but it was worth it. After all, money wasn't a problem—not when we had just come from Philadelphia.

*

The big sign read "PX," but it wasn't big enough to hide an older sign underneath that said "Macy's." I looked it over from across the street.

Somebody had organized it pretty well. I had to admire them. I mean I don't like New York—wouldn't live there if you gave me the place—but it showed a sort of go-getting spirit. It was no easy job getting a full staff together to run a department store operation, when any city the size of New York must have a couple thousand stores. You know what I mean? It's like running a hotel or anything else—how are you going to get people to work for you when they can just as easily walk down the street, find a vacant store and set up their own operation?

But Macy's was fully manned. There was a guard at every door and a walking patrol along the block-front between the entrances to make sure nobody broke in through the windows. They all wore green armbands and uniforms—well, lots of people wore uniforms.

I walked over.

"Afternoon," I said affably to the guard. "I want to pick up some stuff. Typewriter, maybe a gun, you know. How do you work it here? Flat rate for all you can carry, prices marked on everything, or what is it?"

He stared at me suspiciously. He was a monster; six inches taller than I, he must have weighed two hundred and fifty pounds. He didn't look very smart, which might explain why he was working for somebody else these days. But he was smart enough for what he had to do.

He demanded: "You new in town?"

I nodded.

He thought for a minute. "All right, buddy. Go on in. You pick out what you want, see? We'll straighten out the price when you come out."

"Fair enough." I started past him.

He grabbed me by the arm. "No tricks," he ordered. "You come out the same door you went in, understand?"

"Sure," I said, "if that's the way you want it."

That figured—one way or another: either they got a commission, or, like everybody else, they lived on what they could knock down. I filed that for further consideration.

Inside, the store smelled pretty bad. It wasn't just rot, though there was plenty of that; it was musty and stale and old. It was dark, or nearly. About one light in twenty was turned on, in order to conserve power. Naturally the escalators and so on weren't running at all.

*

I passed a counter with pencils and ball-point pens in a case. Most of them were gone—somebody hadn't bothered to go around in back and had simply knocked the glass out—but I found one that worked and an old order pad to write on. Over by the elevators there was a store directory, so I went over and checked it, making a list of the departments worth visiting.

Office Supplies would be the typewriter. Garden & Home was a good bet—maybe I could find a little wheelbarrow to save carrying the typewriter in my arms. What I wanted was one of the big ones where all the keys are solenoid-operated instead of the cam-and-roller arrangement—that was all Arthur could operate. And those things were heavy, as I knew. That was why we had ditched the old one in the Bronx.

Sporting Goods—that would be for a gun, if there were any left. Naturally, they were about the first to go after it happened, when *everybody* wanted a gun. I mean everybody who lived through it. I thought about clothes—it was pretty hot in New York—and decided I might as well take a look.

Typewriter, clothes, gun, wheelbarrow. I made one more note on the pad—try the tobacco counter, but I didn't have much hope for that. They had used cigarettes for currency around this area for a while, until they got enough bank vaults open to supply big bills. It made cigarettes scarce.

I turned away and noticed for the first time that one of the elevators was stopped on the main floor. The doors were closed, but they were glass doors, and although there wasn't any light inside, I could see the elevator was full. There must have been thirty or forty people in the car when it happened.

I'd been thinking that, if nothing else, these New Yorkers were pretty neat—I mean if you don't count the Bronx. But here were thirty or forty skeletons that nobody had even bothered to clear away.

You call that neat? Right in plain view on the ground floor, where everybody who came into the place would be sure to go—I mean if it had been on one of the upper floors, what difference would it have made?

I began to wish we were out of the city. But naturally that would have to wait until we finished what we came here to do—otherwise, what was the point of coming all the way here in the first place?

*

The tobacco counter was bare. I got the wheelbarrow easily enough—there were plenty of those, all sizes; I picked out a nice light red-and-yellow one with rubber-tired wheel. I rolled it over to Sporting Goods on the same floor, but that didn't work out too well. I found a 30-30 with telescopic sights, only there weren't any cartridges to fit it—or anything else. I took the gun anyway; Engdahl would probably have some extra ammunition.

Men's Clothing was a waste of time, too—I guess these New Yorkers were too lazy to do laundry. But I found the typewriter I wanted.

I put the whole load into the wheelbarrow, along with a couple of odds and ends that caught my eye as I passed through Housewares, and I bumped as gently as I could down the shallow steps of the motionless escalator to the ground floor.

I came down the back way, and that was a mistake. It led me right past the food department. Well, I don't have to tell you what *that* was like, with all the exploded cans and the rats as big as poodles. But I found some cologne and soaked a handkerchief in it, and with that over my nose, and some fast footwork for the rats, I managed to get to one of the doors.

It wasn't the one I had come in, but that was all right. I sized up the guard. He looked smart enough for a little bargaining, but not too smart; and if I didn't like his price, I could always remember that I was supposed to go out the other door.

I said: "Psst!"

When he turned around, I said rapidly: "Listen, this isn't the way I came in, but if you want to do business, it'll be the way I come out."

He thought for a second, and then he smiled craftily and said: "All right, come on."

Well, we haggled. The gun was the big thing—he wanted five thousand for that and he wouldn't come down. The wheelbarrow he was willing to let go for five hundred. And the typewriter—he scowled at the typewriter as though it were contagious.

"What you want that for?" he asked suspiciously. I shrugged.

"Well—" he scratched his head—"a thousand?"

I shook my head.

"Five hundred?"

I kept on shaking.

"All right, all right," he grumbled. "Look, you take the other things for six thousand—including what you got in your pockets that you don't think I know about, see? And I'll throw this in. How about it?"

That was fine as far as I was concerned, but just on principle I pushed him a little further. "Forget it," I said. "I'll give you fifty bills for the lot, take it or leave it. Otherwise I'll walk right down the street to Gimbel's and—"

He guffawed.

"Whats the matter?" I demanded.

"Pal," he said, "you kill me. Stranger in town, hey? You can't go anyplace but here."

"Why not?"

"Account of there *ain't* anyplace else. See, the chief here don't like competition. So we don't have to worry about anybody taking their trade elsewhere, like—we burned all the other places down."

That explained a couple of things. I counted out the money, loaded the stuff back in the wheelbarrow and headed for the Statler; but all the time I was counting and loading, I was talking to Big Brainless; and by the time I was actually on the way, I knew a little more about this "chief."

And that was kind of important, because he was the man we were going to have to know very well.

II

I locked the door of the hotel room. Arthur was peeping out of the suitcase at me.

I said: "I'm back. I got your typewriter." He waved his eye at me.

I took out the little kit of electricians' tools I carried, tipped the typewriter on its back and began sorting out leads. I cut them free from the keyboard, soldered on a ground wire, and began taping the leads to the strands of a yard of forty-ply multiplex cable.

It was a slow and dull job. I didn't have to worry about which solenoid lead went to which strand—Arthur could sort them out. But all the same it took an hour, pretty near, and I was getting hungry by the time I got the last connection taped. I shifted the typewriter so that both Arthur and I could see it, rolled in a sheet of paper and hooked the cable to Arthur's receptors.

Nothing happened.

"Oh," I said. "Excuse me, Arthur. I forgot to plug it in."

I found a wall socket. The typewriter began to hum and then it started to rattle and type:

DURA AUK UKOO RQK MWS AQB

It stopped.

"Come on, Arthur," I ordered impatiently. "Sort them out, will you?"

Laboriously it typed:

!!!

Then, for a time, there was a clacking and thumping as he typed random letters, peeping out of the suitcase to see what he had typed, until the sheet I had put in was used up.

I replaced it and waited, as patiently as I could, smoking one of the last of my cigarettes. After fifteen minutes or so, he had the hang of it pretty well. He typed:

YOU DAMQXXX DAMN FOOL WHUXXX WHY DID YOU LEAQNXXX LEAVE ME ALONE Q Q

"Aw, Arthur," I said. "Use your head, will you? I couldn't carry that old typewriter of yours all the way down through the Bronx. It was getting pretty beat-up. Anyway, I've only got two hands—"

YOU LOUSE, it rattled, ARE YOU TRYONXXX TRYING TO INSULT ME BECAUSE I DONT HAVE ANY Q Q

"Arthur!" I said, shocked. "You know better than that!"

The typewriter slammed its carriage back and forth ferociously a couple of times. Then he said: ALL RIGHT SAM YOU KNOW YOUVE GOT ME BY THE THROAT SO YOU CAN DO ANYTHING YOU WANT TO WITH ME WHO CARES ABOUT MY FEELINGS ANYHOW

"Please don't take that attitude," I coaxed.

WELL

"Please?"

He capitulated. ALL RIGHT SAY HEARD ANYTHING FROM ENGDAHL Q Q

"No."

ISNT THAT JUST LIKE HIM Q Q CANT DEPEND ON THAT MAN HE WAS THE LOUSIEST ELECTRICIANS MATE ON THE SEA SPRITE AND HE ISNT MUCH BETTER NOW SAY SAM REMEMBER WHEN WE HAD TO GET HIM OUT OF THE JUG IN NEWPORT NEWS BECAUSE

I settled back and relaxed. I might as well. That was the trouble with getting Arthur a new typewriter after a couple of days without one—he had so much garrulity stored up in his little brain, and the only person to spill it on was me.

*

Apparently I fell asleep. Well, I mean I must have, because I woke up. I had been dreaming I was on guard post outside the Yard at Portsmouth, and it was night, and I looked up and there was something up there, all silvery and bad. It was a missile—and that was silly, because you never see a missile. But this was a dream.

And the thing burst, like a Roman candle flaring out, all sorts of comet-trails of light, and then the whole sky was full of bright and colored snow. Little tiny flakes of light coming down, a mist of light, radiation dropping like dew; and it was so pretty, and I took a deep breath. And my lungs burned out like slow fire, and I coughed myself to death with the explosions of the missile banging against my flaming ears. . . .

Well, it was a dream. It probably wasn't like that at all—and if it had been, I wasn't there to see it, because I was tucked away safe under a hundred and twenty fathoms of Atlantic water. All of us were on the *Sea Sprite*.

But it was a bad dream and it bothered me, even when I woke up and found that the banging explosions of the missile were the noise of Arthur's typewriter carriage crashing furiously back and forth.

He peeped out of the suitcase and saw that I was awake. He demanded: HOW CAN YOU FALL ASLEEP WHEN WERE IN A PLACE LIKE THIS Q Q ANYTHING COULD HAPPEN SAM I KNOW YOU DONT CARE WHAT HAPPENS TO ME BUT FOR YOUR OWN SAKE YOU SHOULDNT

"Oh, dry up," I said.

Being awake, I remembered that I was hungry. There was still no sign of Engdahl or the others, but that wasn't too surprising—they hadn't known exactly when we would arrive. I wished I had thought to bring some food back to the room. It looked like long waiting and I wouldn't want to leave Arthur alone again—after all, he was partly right.

I thought of the telephone.

On the off-chance that it might work, I picked it up. Amazing, a voice from the desk answered.

I crossed my fingers and said: "Room service?"

And the voice answered amiably enough: "Hold on, buddy. I'll see if they answer."

Clicking and a good long wait. Then a new voice said: "Whaddya want?"

There was no sense pressing my luck by asking for anything like a complete meal. I would be lucky if I got a sandwich.

I said: "Please, may I have a Spam sandwich on Rye Krisp and some coffee for Room Fifteen Forty-one?"

"Please, you go to hell!" the voice snarled. "What do you think this is, some damn delicatessen? You want liquor, we'll get you liquor. That's what room service is for!"

*

I hung up. What was the use of arguing? Arthur was clacking peevishly:

WHATS THE MATTER SAM YOU THINKING OF YOUR BELLY AGAIN Q Q

"You would be if you—" I started, and then I stopped. Arthur's feelings were delicate enough already. I mean suppose that all you had left of what you were born with was a brain in a kind of sardine can, wouldn't you be sensitive? Well, Arthur was more sensitive than you would be, believe me. Of course, it was his own foolish fault—I mean you don't get a prosthetic tank unless you die by accident, or something like that, because if it's disease they usually can't save even the brain.

The phone rang again.

It was the desk clerk. "Say, did you get what you wanted?" he asked chummily.

"No."

"Oh. Too bad," he said, but cheerfully. "Listen, buddy, I forgot to tell you before. That Miss Engdahl you were expecting, she's on her way up."

I dropped the phone onto the cradle.

"Arthur!" I yelled. "Keep quiet for a while—trouble!"

He clacked once, and the typewriter shut itself off. I jumped for the door of the bathroom, cursing the fact that I didn't have cartridges for the gun. Still, empty or not, it would have to do.

I ducked behind the bathroom door, in the shadows, covering the hall door. Because there were two things wrong with what the desk clerk had told me. Vern Engdahl wasn't a "miss," to begin with; and whatever name he used when he came to call on me, it wouldn't be Vern Engdahl.

There was a knock on the door. I called: "Come in!"

The door opened and the girl who called herself Vern Engdahl came in slowly, looking around. I stayed quiet and out of sight until she was all the way in. She didn't seem to be armed; there wasn't anyone with her.

I stepped out, holding the gun on her. Her eyes opened wide and she seemed about to turn.

"Hold it! Come on in, you. Close the door!"

She did. She looked as though she were expecting me. I looked her over—medium pretty, not very tall, not very plump, not very old. I'd have guessed twenty or so, but that's not my line of work; she could have been almost any age from seventeen on.

The typewriter switched itself on and began to pound agitatedly. I crossed over toward her and paused to peer at what Arthur was yacking about: SEARCH HER YOU DAMN FOOL MAYBE SHES GOT A GUN

I ordered: "Shut up, Arthur. I'm *going* to search her. You! Turn around!"

*

She shrugged and turned around, her hands in the air. Over her shoulder, she said: "You're taking this all wrong, Sam. I came here to make a deal with you."

"Sure you did."

But her knowing my name was a blow, too. I mean what was the use of all that sneaking around if people in New York were going to know we were here?

I walked up close behind her and patted what there was to pat. There didn't seem to be a gun.

"You tickle," she complained.

I took her pocketbook away from her and went through it. No gun. A lot of money—an *awful* lot of money. I mean there must have been two or three hundred thousand dollars. There was nothing with a name on it in the pocketbook.

She said: "Can I put my hands down, Sam?"

"In a minute." I thought for a second and then decided to do it—you know, I just couldn't afford to take chances. I cleared my throat and ordered: "Take off your clothes."

Her head jerked around and she stared at me. "*What?*"

"Take them off. You heard me."

"Now wait a minute—" she began dangerously.

I said: "Do what I tell you, hear? How do I know you haven't got a knife tucked away?"

She clenched her teeth. "Why, you dirty little man! What do you think—" Then she shrugged. She looked at me with contempt and said: "All right. What's the difference?"

Well, there was a considerable difference. She began to unzip and unbutton and wriggle, and pretty soon she was standing there in her underwear, looking at me as though I were a two-headed worm. It was interesting, but kind of embarrassing. I could see Arthur's eye-stalk waving excitedly out of the opened suitcase.

I picked up her skirt and blouse and shook them. I could feel myself blushing, and there didn't seem to be anything in them.

I growled: "Okay, I guess that's enough. You can put your clothes back on now."

"Gee, thanks," she said.

She looked at me thoughtfully and then shook her head as if she'd never seen anything like me before and never hoped to again. Without another word, she began to get back into her clothes. I had to admire her poise. I mean she was perfectly calm about the whole thing. You'd have thought she was used to taking her clothes off in front of strange men.

Well, for that matter, maybe she was; but it wasn't any of my business.

*

Arthur was clacking distractedly, but I didn't pay any attention to him. I demanded: "All right, now who are you and what do you want?"

She pulled up a stocking and said: "You couldn't have asked me that in the first place, could you? I'm Vern Eng—"

"*Cut it out!*"

She stared at me. "I was only going to say I'm Vern Engdahl's partner. We've got a little business deal cooking and I wanted to talk to you about this proposition."

Arthur squawked: WHATS ENGDAHL UP TO NOW Q Q SAM IM WARNING YOU I DONT LIKE THE LOOK OF THIS THIS WOMAN AND ENGDAHL ARE PROBABLY DOUBLECROSSING US

I said: "All right, Arthur, relax. I'm taking care of things. Now start over, you. What's your name?"

She finished putting on her shoe and stood up. "Amy."

"Last name?"

She shrugged and fished in her purse for a cigarette. "What does it matter? Mind if I sit down?"

"Go ahead," I rumbled. "But don't stop talking!"

"Oh," she said, "we've got plenty of time to straighten things out." She lit the cigarette and walked over to the chair by the window. On the way, she gave the luggage a good long look.

Arthur's eyestalk cowered back into the suitcase as she came close. She winked at me, grinned, bent down and peered inside.

"My," she said, "he's a nice shiny one, isn't he?"

The typewriter began to clatter frantically. I didn't even bother to look; I told him: "Arthur, if you can't keep quiet, you have to expect people to know you're there."

She sat down and crossed her legs. "Now then," she said. "Frankly, he's what I came to see you about. Vern told me you had a pross. I want to buy it."

The typewriter thrashed its carriage back and forth furiously.

"Arthur isn't for sale."

"No?" She leaned back. "Vern's already sold me his interest, you know. And you don't really have any choice. You see, I'm in charge of materiel procurement for the Major. If you want to sell your share, fine. If you don't, why, we requisition it anyhow. Do you follow?"

I was getting irritated—at Vern Engdahl, for whatever the hell he thought he was doing; but at her because she was handy. I shook my head.

"Fifty thousand dollars? I mean for your interest?"

"No."

"Seventy-five?"

"No!"

"Oh, come on now. A hundred thousand?"

It wasn't going to make any impression on her, but I tried to explain: "Arthur's a friend of mine. He isn't for sale."

*

She shook her head. "What's the matter with you? Engdahl wasn't like this. He sold his interest for forty thousand and was glad to get it."

Clatter-clatter-clatter from Arthur. I didn't blame him for having hurt feelings that time.

Amy said in a discouraged tone: "Why can't people be reasonable? The Major doesn't like it when people aren't reasonable."

I lowered the gun and cleared my throat. "He doesn't?" I asked, cuing her. I wanted to hear more about this Major, who seemed to have the city pretty well under his thumb.

"No, he doesn't." She shook her head sorrowfully. She said in an accusing voice: "You out-of-towners don't know what it's like to try to run a city the size of New York. There are fifteen thousand people here, do you know that? It isn't one of your hick towns. And it's worry, worry, worry all the time, trying to keep things going."

"I bet," I said sympathetically. "You're, uh, pretty close to the Major?"

She said stiffly: "I'm not married to him, if that's what you mean. Though I've had my chances. . . . But you see how it is. Fifteen thousand people to run a place the size of New York! It's forty men to operate the power station, and twenty-five on the PX, and thirty on the hotel here. And then there are the local groceries, and the Army, and the Coast Guard, and the Air Force—though, really, that's only two men—and—Well, you get the picture."

"I certainly do. Look, what kind of a guy *is* the Major?"

She shrugged. "A guy."

"I mean what does he like?"

"Women, mostly," she said, her expression clouded. "Come on now. What about it?"

I stalled. "What do you want Arthur for?"

She gave me a disgusted look. "What do you think? To relieve the manpower shortage, naturally. There's more work than there are men. Now if the Major could just get hold of a couple of prosthetics, like this thing here, why, he could put them in the big installations. This one used to be an engineer or something, Vern said."

"Well . . . *like* an engineer."

*

Amy shrugged. "So why couldn't we connect him up with the power station? It's been done. The Major knows that—he was in the Pentagon when they switched all the aircraft warning net over from computer to prosthetic control. So why couldn't we do the same thing with our power station and release forty men for other assignments? This thing could work day, night, Sundays—what's the difference when you're just a brain in a sardine can?"

Clatter-rattle-*bang*.

She looked startled. "Oh. I forgot he was listening."

"No deal," I said.

She said: "A hundred and fifty thousand?"

A hundred and fifty thousand dollars. I considered that for a while. Arthur clattered warningly.

"Well," I temporized, "I'd have to be sure he was getting into good hands—"

The typewriter thrashed wildly. The sheet of paper fluttered out of the carriage. He'd used it up. Automatically I picked it up—it was covered with imprecations, self-pity and threats—and started to put a new one in.

"No," I said, bending over the typewriter, "I guess I couldn't sell him. It just wouldn't be right—"

That was my mistake; it was the wrong time for me to say that, because I had taken my eyes off her.

The room bent over and clouted me.

I half turned, not more than a fraction conscious, and I saw this Amy girl, behind me, with the shoe still in her hand, raised to give me another blackjacking on the skull.

The shoe came down, and it must have weighed more than it looked, and even the fractional bit of consciousness went crashing away.

III

I have to tell you about Vern Engdahl. We were all from the *Sea Sprite*, of course—me and Vern and even Arthur. The thing about Vern is that he was the lowest-ranking one of us all—only an electricians' mate third, I mean when anybody paid any attention to things like that—and yet he was pretty much doing the thinking for the rest of us. Coming to New York was his idea—he told us that was the only place we could get what we wanted.

Well, as long as we were carrying Arthur along with us, we pretty much needed Vern, because he was the one who knew how to keep the lash-up going. You've got no idea what kind of pumps and plumbing go into a prosthetic tank until you've seen one opened up. And, naturally, Arthur didn't want any breakdowns without somebody around to fix things up.

The *Sea Sprite*, maybe you know, was one of the old liquid-sodium-reactor subs—too slow for combat duty, but as big as a barn, so they made it a hospital ship. We were cruising deep when the missiles hit, and, of course, when we came up, there wasn't much for a hospital ship to do. I mean there isn't any sense fooling around with anybody who's taken a good deep breath of fallout.

So we went back to Newport News to see what had happened. And we found out what had happened. And there wasn't anything much to do except pay off the crew and let them go. But us three stuck together. Why not? It wasn't as if we had any families to go back to any more.

Vern just loved all this stuff—he'd been an Eagle Scout; maybe that had something to do with it—and he showed us how to boil drinking water and forage in the woods and all like that, because nobody in his right mind wanted to go near any kind of a town, until the cold weather set in, anyway. And it was always Vern, Vern, telling us what to do, ironing out our troubles.

It worked out, except that there was this one thing. Vern had bright ideas. But he didn't always tell us what they were.

So I wasn't so very surprised when I came to. I mean there I was, tied up, with this girl Amy standing over me, holding the gun like a club. Evidently she'd found out that there weren't any cartridges. And in a couple of minutes there was a knock on the door, and she yelled, "Come in," and in came Vern. And the man who was with him had to be somebody important, because there were eight or ten other men crowding in close behind.

I didn't need to look at the oak leaves on his shoulders to realize that here was the chief, the fellow who ran this town, the Major.

It was just the kind of thing Vern *would* do.

*

Vern said, with the look on his face that made strange officers wonder why this poor persecuted man had been forced to spend so much time in the brig: "Now, Major, I'm sure we can straighten all this out. Would you mind leaving me alone with my friend here for a moment?"

The Major teetered on his heels, thinking. He was a tall, youngish-bald type, with a long, worried, horselike face. He said: "Ah, do you think we should?"

"I guarantee there'll be no trouble, Major," Vern promised.

The Major pulled at his little mustache. "Very well," he said. "Amy, you come along."

"We'll be right here, Major," Vern said reassuringly, escorting him to the door.

"You bet you will," said the Major, and tittered. "Ah, bring that gun along with you, Amy. And be sure this man knows that we have bullets."

They closed the door. Arthur had been cowering in his suitcase, but now his eyestalk peeped out and the rattling and clattering from that typewriter sounded like the Battle of the Bulge.

I demanded: "Come on, Vern. What's this all about?"

Vern said: "How much did they offer you?"

Clatter-bang-BANG. I peeked, and Arthur was saying: WARNED YOU SAM THAT ENGDAHL WAS UP TO TRICKS PLEASE SAM PLEASE PLEASE PLEASE HIT HIM ON THE HEAD KNOCK HIM OUT HE MUST HAVE A GUN SO GET IT AND SHOOT OUR WAY OUT OF HERE

"A hundred and fifty thousand dollars," I said.

Vern looked outraged. "I only got forty!"

Arthur clattered: VERN I APPEAL TO YOUR COMMON DECENCY WERE OLD SHIPMATES VERN REMEMBER ALL THE TIMES I

"Still," Vern mused, "it's all common funds anyway, right? Arthur belongs to both of us."

I DONT DONT DONT REPEAT DONT BELONG TO ANYBODY BUT ME

"That's true," I said grudgingly. "But I carried him, remember."

SAM WHATS THE MATTER WITH YOU Q Q I DONT LIKE THE EXPRESSION ON YOUR FACE LISTEN SAM YOU ARENT

Vern said, "A hundred and fifty thousand, remember."

THINKING OF SELLING

"And of course we couldn't get out of here," Vern pointed out. "They've got us surrounded."

ME TO THESE RATS Q Q SAM VERN PLEASE DONT SCARE ME

*

I said, pointing to the fluttering paper in the rattling machine: "You're worrying our friend."

Vern shrugged impatiently.

I KNEW I SHOULDNT HAVE TRUSTED YOU, Arthur wept. THATS ALL I MEAN TO YOU EH

Vern said: "Well, Sam? Let's take the cash and get this thing over with. After all, he *will* have the best of treatment."

It was a little like selling your sister into white slavery, but what else was there to do? Besides, I kind of trusted Vern.

"All right," I said.

What Arthur said nearly scorched the paper.

Vern helped pack Arthur up for moving. I mean it was just a matter of pulling the plugs out and making sure he had a fresh battery, but Vern wanted to supervise it himself. Because one of the little things Vern had up his sleeve was that he had found a spot for himself on the Major's payroll. He was now the official Prosthetic (Human) Maintenance Department Chief.

The Major said to me: "Ah, Dunlap. What sort of experience have you had?"

"Experience?"

"In the Navy. Your friend Engdahl suggested you might want to join us here."

"Oh. I see what you mean." I shook my head. "Nothing that would do you any good, I'm afraid. I was a yeoman."

"Yeoman?"

"Like a company clerk," I explained. "I mean I kept records and cut orders and made out reports and all like that."

"Company clerk!" The eyes in the long horsy face gleamed. "Ah, you're mistaken, Dunlap! Why, that's *just* what we need. Our morning reports are in foul shape. Foul! Come over to HQ. Lieutenant Bankhead will give you a lift."

"Lieutenant Bankhead?"

I got an elbow in my ribs for that. It was that girl Amy, standing alongside me. "I," she said, "am Lieutenant Bankhead."

Well, I went along with her, leaving Engdahl and Arthur behind. But I must admit I wasn't sure of my reception.

Out in front of the hotel was a whole fleet of cars—three or four of them, at least. There was a big old Cadillac that looked like a gangsters' car—thick glass in the windows, tires that looked like they belonged on a truck. I was willing to bet it was bulletproof and also that it belonged to the Major. I was right both times. There was a little MG with the top down, and a couple of light trucks. Every one of them was painted bright orange, and every one of them had the star-and-bar of the good old United States Army on its side.

It took me back to old times—all but the unmilitary color. Amy led me to the MG and pointed.

"Sit," she said.

I sat. She got in the other side and we were off.

It was a little uncomfortable on account of I wasn't just sure whether I ought to apologize for making her take her clothes off. And then she tramped on the gas of that little car and I didn't think much about being embarrassed or about her black lace lingerie. I was only thinking about one thing—how to stay alive long enough to get out of that car.

IV

See, what we really wanted was an ocean liner.

The rest of us probably would have been happy enough to stay in Lehigh County, but Arthur was getting restless.

He was a terrible responsibility, in a way. I suppose there were a hundred thousand people or so left in the country, and not more than forty or fifty of them were like Arthur—I mean if you want to call a man in a prosthetic tank a "person." But we all did. We'd got pretty used to him. We'd shipped together in the war—and survived together, as a few of the actual fighters did, those who were lucky enough to be underwater or high in the air when the ICBMs landed—and as few civilians did.

I mean there wasn't much chance for surviving, for anybody who happened to be breathing the open air when it happened. I mean you can do just so much about making a "clean" H-bomb, and if you cut out the long-life fission products, the short-life ones get pretty deadly.

Anyway, there wasn't much damage, except of course that everybody was dead. All the surface vessels lost their crews. All the population of the cities were gone. And so then, when Arthur slipped on the gangplank coming into Newport News and broke his fool neck, why, we had the whole staff of the *Sea Sprite* to work on him. I mean what else did the surgeons have to do?

Of course, that was a long time ago.

But we'd stayed together. We headed for the farm country around Allentown, Pennsylvania, because Arthur and Vern Engdahl claimed to know it pretty well. I think maybe they had some hope of finding family or friends, but naturally there wasn't any of that. And when you got into the inland towns, there hadn't been much of an attempt to clean them up. At least the big cities and the ports had been gone over, in some spots anyway, by burial squads. Although when we finally decided to move out and went to Philadelphia—

Well, let's be fair; there had been fighting around there after the big fight. Anyway, that wasn't so very uncommon. That was one of the reasons that for a long time—four or five years, at any rate—we stayed away from big cities.

We holed up in a big farmhouse in Lehigh County. It had its own generator from a little stream, and that took care of Arthur's power needs; and the previous occupants had been just crazy about stashing away food. There was enough to last a century, and that took care of the two of us. We appreciated that. We even took the old folks out and gave them a decent burial. I mean they'd all been in the family car, so we just had to tow it to a gravel pit and push it in.

The place had its own well, with an electric pump and a hot-water system—oh, it was nice. I was sorry to leave but, frankly, Arthur was driving us nuts.

We never could make the television work—maybe there weren't any stations near enough. But we pulled in a couple of radio stations pretty well and Arthur got a big charge out of listening to them—see, he could hear four or five at a time and I suppose that made him feel better than the rest of us.

He heard that the big cities were cleaned up and every one of them seemed to want immigrants—they were pleading, pleading all the time, like the TV-set and vacuum-cleaner people used to in the old days; they guaranteed we'd like it if we only came to live in Philly, or Richmond, or Baltimore, or wherever. And I guess Arthur kind of hoped we might find another pross. And then—well, Engdahl came up with this idea of an ocean liner.

It figured. I mean you get out in the middle of the ocean and what's the difference what it's like on land? And it especially appealed to Arthur because he wanted to do some surface sailing. He never had when he was real—I mean when he had arms and legs like anybody else. He'd gone right into the undersea service the minute he got out of school.

And—well, sailing was what Arthur knew something about and I suppose even a prosthetic man wants to feel useful. It was like Amy said: He could be hooked up to an automated factory—

Or to a ship.

*

HQ for the Major's Temporary Military Government—that's what the sign said—was on the 91st floor of the Empire State Building, and right there that tells you something about the man. I mean you know how much power it takes to run those elevators all the way up to the top? But the Major must have liked being able to look down on everybody else.

Amy Bankhead conducted me to his office and sat me down to wait for His Military Excellency to arrive. She filled me in on him, to some degree. He'd been an absolute nothing before the war; but he had a reserve commission in the Air Force, and when things began to look sticky, they'd called him up and put him in a Missile Master control point, underground somewhere up around Ossining.

He was the duty officer when it happened, and naturally he hadn't noticed anything like an enemy aircraft, and naturally the anti-missile missiles were still rusting in their racks all around the city; but since the place had been operating on sealed ventilation, the duty complement could stay there until the short half-life radioisotopes wore themselves out.

And then the Major found out that he was not only in charge of the fourteen men and women of his division at the center—he was ranking United States Military Establishment officer farther than the eye could see. So he beat it, fast as he could, for New York, because what Army officer doesn't dream about being stationed in New York? And he set up his Temporary Military Government—and that was nine years ago.

If there hadn't been plenty to go around, I don't suppose he would have lasted a week—none of these city chiefs would have. But as things were, he was in on the ground floor, and as newcomers trickled into the city, his boys already had things nicely organized.

It was a soft touch.

*

Well, we were about a week getting settled in New York and things were looking pretty good. Vern calmed me down by pointing out that, after all, we had to sell Arthur, and hadn't we come out of it plenty okay?

And we had. There was no doubt about it. Not only did we have a fat price for Arthur, which was useful because there were a lot of things we would have to buy, but we both had jobs working for the Major.

Vern was his specialist in the care and feeding of Arthur and I was his chief of office routine—and, as such, I delighted his fussy little soul, because by adding what I remembered of Navy protocol to what he was able to teach me of Army routine, we came up with as snarled a mass of red tape as any field-grade officer in the whole history of all armed forces had been able to accumulate. Oh, I tell you, nobody sneezed in New York without a report being made out in triplicate, with eight endorsements.

Of course there wasn't anybody to send them to, but that didn't stop the Major. He said with determination: "Nobody's ever going to chew *me* out for non-compliance with regulations—even if I have to invent the regulations myself!"

We set up in a bachelor apartment on Central Park South—the Major had the penthouse; the whole building had been converted to barracks—and the first chance we got, Vern snaffled some transportation and we set out to find an ocean liner.

See, the thing was that an ocean liner isn't easy to steal. I mean we'd scouted out the lay of the land before we ever entered the city itself, and there were plenty of liners, but there wasn't one that looked like we could just jump in and sail it away. For that we needed an organization. Since we didn't have one, the best thing to do was borrow the Major's.

Vern turned up with Amy Bankhead's MG, and he also turned up with Amy. I can't say I was displeased, because I was beginning to like the girl; but did you ever try to ride three people in the seats of an MG? Well, the way to do it is by having one passenger sit in the other passenger's lap, which would have been all right except that Amy insisted on driving.

We headed downtown and over to the West Side. The Major's Topographical Section—one former billboard artist—had prepared road maps with little red-ink Xs marking the streets that were blocked, which was most of the streets; but we charted a course that would take us where we wanted to go. Thirty-fourth Street was open, and so was Fifth Avenue all of its length, so we scooted down Fifth, crossed over, got under the Elevated Highway and whined along uptown toward the Fifties.

"There's one," cried Amy, pointing.

I was on Vern's lap, so I was making the notes. It was a Fruit Company combination freighter-passenger vessel. I looked at Vern, and Vern shrugged as best he could, so I wrote it down; but it wasn't exactly what we wanted. No, not by a long shot.

*

Still, the thing to do was to survey our resources, and then we could pick the one we liked best. We went all the way up to the end of the big-ship docks, and then turned and came back down, all the way to the Battery. It wasn't pleasure driving, exactly—half a dozen times we had to get out the map and detour around impenetrable jams of stalled and empty cars—or anyway, if they weren't exactly empty, the people in them were no longer in shape to get out of our way. But we made it.

We counted sixteen ships in dock that looked as though they might do for our purposes. We had to rule out the newer ones and the reconverted jobs. I mean, after all, U-235 just lasts so long, and you can steam around the world on a walnut-shell of it, or whatever it is, but you can't store it. So we had to stick with the ships that were powered with conventional fuel—and, on consideration, only oil at that.

But that left sixteen, as I say. Some of them, though, had suffered visibly from being left untended for nearly a decade, so that for our purposes they might as well have been abandoned in the middle of the Atlantic; we didn't have the equipment or ambition to do any great amount of salvage work.

The *Empress of Britain* would have been a pretty good bet, for instance, except that it was lying at pretty nearly a forty-five-degree angle in its berth. So was the *United States*, and so was the *Caronia*. The *Stockholm* was straight enough, but I took a good look, and only one tier of portholes was showing above the water—evidently it had settled nice and even, but it was on the bottom all the same. Well, that mud sucks with a fine tight grip, and we weren't going to try to loosen it.

All in all, eleven of the sixteen ships were out of commission just from what we could see driving by.

Vern and I looked at each other. We stood by the MG, while Amy sprawled her legs over the side and waited for us to make up our minds.

"Not good, Sam," said Vern, looking worried.

I said: "Well, that still leaves five. There's the *Vulcania*, the *Cristobal*—"

"Too small."

"All right. The *Manhattan*, the *Liberté* and the *Queen Elizabeth*."

Amy looked up, her eyes gleaming. "Where's the question?" she demanded. "Naturally, it's the *Queen*."

I tried to explain. "Please, Amy. Leave these things to us, will you?"

"But the Major won't settle for anything but the best!"

"The *Major*?"

*

I glanced at Vern, who wouldn't meet my eyes. "Well," I said, "look at the problems, Amy. First we have to check it over. Maybe it's been burned out—how do we know? Maybe the channel isn't even deep enough to float it any more—how do we know? Where are we going to get the oil for it?"

"We'll get the oil," Amy said cheerfully.

"And what if the channel isn't deep enough?"

"She'll float," Amy promised. "At high tide, anyway. Even if the channel hasn't been dredged in ten years."

I shrugged and gave up. What was the use of arguing?

We drove back to the *Queen Elizabeth* and I had to admit that there was a certain attraction about that big old dowager. We all got out and strolled down the pier, looking over as much as we could see.

The pier had never been cleaned out. It bothered me a little—I mean I don't like skeletons much—but Amy didn't seem to mind.

The *Queen* must have just docked when it happened, because you could still see bony queues, as though they were waiting for customs inspection.

Some of the bags had been opened and the contents scattered around—naturally, somebody was bound to think of looting the *Queen*. But there were as many that hadn't been touched as that had been opened, and the whole thing had the look of an amateur attempt. And that was all to the good, because the fewer persons who had boarded the *Queen* in the decade since it happened, the more chance of our finding it in usable shape.

Amy saw a gangplank still up, and with cries of girlish glee ran aboard.

I plucked at Vern's sleeve. "You," I said. "What's this about what the *Major* won't settle for less than?"

He said: "Aw, Sam, I had to tell her something, didn't I?"

"But what about the Major—"

He said patiently: "You don't understand. It's all part of my plan, see? The Major is the big thing here and he's got a birthday coming up next month. Well, the way I put it to Amy, we'll fix him up with a yacht as a birthday present, see? And, of course, when it's all fixed up and ready to lift anchor—"

I said doubtfully: "That's the hard way, Vern. Why couldn't we just sort of get steam up and take off?"

He shook his head. "*That* is the hard way. This way we get all the help and supplies we need, understand?"

I shrugged. That was the way it was, so what was the use of arguing?

But there was one thing more on my mind. I said: "How come Amy's so interested in making the Major happy?"

Vern chortled. "Jealous, eh?"

"I asked a question!"

"Calm down, boy. It's just that he's in charge of things here so naturally she wants to keep in good with him."

I scowled. "I keep hearing stories about how the Major's chief interest in life is women. You sure she isn't ambitious to be one of them?"

He said: "The reason she wants to keep him happy is so she *won't* be one of them."

V

The name of the place was Bayonne.

Vern said: "One of them's *got* to have oil, Sam. It *has* to."

"Sure," I said.

"There's no question about it. Look, this is where the tankers came to discharge oil. They'd come in here, pump the oil into the refinery tanks and—"

"Vern," I said. "Let's look, shall we?"

He shrugged, and we hopped off the little outboard motorboat onto a landing stage. The tankers towered over us, rusty and screeching as the waves rubbed them against each other.

There were fifty of them there at least, and we poked around them for hours. The hatches were rusted shut and unmanageable, but you could tell a lot by sniffing. Gasoline odor was out; smell of seaweed and dead fish was out; but the heavy, rank smell of fuel oil, that was what we were sniffing for. Crews had been aboard these ships when the missiles came, and crews were still aboard.

Beyond the two-part superstructures of the tankers, the skyline of New York was visible. I looked up, sweating, and saw the Empire State Building and imagined Amy up there, looking out toward us.

She knew we were here. It was her idea. She had scrounged up a naval engineer, or what she called a naval engineer—he had once been a stoker on a ferryboat. But he claimed he knew what he was talking about when he said the only thing the *Queen* needed to make 'er go was oil. And so we left him aboard to tinker and polish, with a couple of helpers Amy detached from the police force, and we tackled the oil problem.

Which meant Bayonne. Which was where we were.

It had to be a tanker with at least a fair portion of its cargo intact, because the *Queen* was a thirsty creature, drinking fuel not by the shot or gallon but by the ton.

"Saaam! Sam *Dunlap*!"

I looked up, startled. Five ships away, across the U of the mooring, Vern Engdahl was bellowing at me through cupped hands.

"I found it!" he shouted. "Oil, lots of oil! Come look!"

I clasped my hands over my head and looked around. It was a long way around to the tanker Vern was on, hopping from deck to deck, detouring around open stretches.

I shouted: "I'll get the boat!"

He waved and climbed up on the rail of the ship, his feet dangling over, looking supremely happy and pleased with himself. He lit a cigarette, leaned back against the upward sweep of the rail and waited.

It took me a little time to get back to the boat and a little more time than that to get the damn motor started. Vern! "Let's not take that lousy little twelve horse-power, Sam," he'd said reasonably. "The twenty-five's more what we need!" And maybe it was, but none of the motors had been started in most of a decade, and the twenty-five was just that much harder to start now.

I struggled over it, swearing, for twenty minutes or more.

The tanker by whose side we had tied up began to swing toward me as the tide changed to outgoing.

*

For a moment there, I was counting seconds, expecting to have to make a jump for it before the big red steel flank squeezed the little outboard flat against the piles.

But I got it started—just about in time. I squeezed out of the trap with not much more than a yard to spare and threaded my way into open water.

There was a large, threatening sound, like an enormous slow cough.

I rounded the stern of the last tanker between me and open water, and looked into the eye of a fire-breathing dragon.

Vern and his cigarettes! The tanker was loose and ablaze, bearing down on me with the slow drift of the ebbing tide. From the hatches on the forward deck, two fountains of fire spurted up and out, like enormous nostrils spouting flame. The hawsers had been burned through, the ship was adrift, I was in its path—

And so was the frantically splashing figure of Vern Engdahl, trying desperately to swim out of the way in the water before it.

What kept it from blowing up in our faces I will never know, unless it was the pressure in the tanks forcing the flame out; but it didn't. Not just then. Not until I had Engdahl aboard and we were out in the middle of the Hudson, staring back; and then it went up all right, all at once, like a missile or a volcano; and there had been fifty tankers in that one mooring, but there weren't any any more, or not in shape for us to use.

I looked at Engdahl.

He said defensively: "Honest, Sam, I thought it was oil. It *smelled* like oil. How was I to know—"

"Shut up," I said.

He shrugged, injured. "But it's all right, Sam. No fooling. There are plenty of other tankers around. Plenty. Down toward the Amboys, maybe moored out in the channel. There must be. We'll find them."

"No," I said. "*You* will."

And that was all I said, because I am forgiving by nature; but I thought a great deal more.

Surprisingly, though, he did find a tanker with a full load, the very next day.

It became a question of getting the tanker to the *Queen*. I left that part up to Vern, since he claimed to be able to handle it.

It took him two weeks. First it was finding the tanker, then it was locating a tug in shape to move, then it was finding someone to pilot the tug. Then it was waiting for a clear and windless day—because the pilot he found had got all his experience sailing Star boats on Long Island Sound—and then it was easing the tanker out of Newark Bay, into the channel, down to the pier in the North River—

Oh, it was work and no fooling. I enjoyed it very much, because I didn't have to do it.

*

But I had enough to keep me busy at that. I found a man who claimed he used to be a radio engineer. And if he was an engineer, I was Albert Einstein's mother, but at least he knew which end of a soldering iron was hot. There was no need for any great skill, since there weren't going to be very many vessels to communicate with.

Things began to move.

The advantage of a ship like the *Queen*, for our purposes, was that the thing was pretty well automated to start out with. I mean never mind what the seafaring unions required in the way of flesh-and-blood personnel. What it came down to was that one man in the bridge or wheelhouse could pretty well make any part of the ship go or not go.

The engine-room telegraph wasn't hooked up to control the engines, no. But the wiring diagram needed only a few little changes to get the same effect, because where in the original concept a human being would take a look at the repeater down in the engine room, nod wisely, and push a button that would make the engines stop, start, or whatever—why, all we had to do was cut out the middleman, so to speak.

Our genius of the soldering iron replaced flesh and blood with some wiring and, presto, we had centralized engine control.

The steering was even easier. Steering was a matter of electronic control and servomotors to begin with. Windjammers in the old movies might have a man lashed to the wheel whose muscle power turned the rudder, but, believe me, a big superliner doesn't. The rudders weigh as much as any old windjammer ever did from stem to stern; you have to have motors to turn them; and it was only a matter of getting out the old soldering iron again.

By the time we were through, we had every operational facility of the *Queen* hooked up to a single panel on the bridge.

Engdahl showed up with the oil tanker just about the time we got the wiring complete. We rigged up a pump and filled the bunkers till they were topped off full. We guessed, out of hope and ignorance, that there was enough in there to take us half a dozen times around the world at normal cruising speed, and maybe there was. Anyway, it didn't matter, for surely we had enough to take us anywhere we wanted to go, and then there would be more.

We crossed our fingers, turned our ex-ferry-stoker loose, pushed a button—

Smoke came out of the stacks.

The antique screws began to turn over. Astern, a sort of hump of muddy water appeared. The *Queen* quivered underfoot. The mooring hawsers creaked and sang.

"Turn her off!" screamed Engdahl. "She's headed for Times Square!"

Well, that was an exaggeration, but not much of one; and there wasn't any sense in stirring up the bottom mud. I pushed buttons and the screws stopped. I pushed another button, and the big engines quietly shut themselves off, and in a few moments the stacks stopped puffing their black smoke.

The ship was alive.

Solemnly Engdahl and I shook hands. We had the thing licked. All, that is, except for the one small problem of Arthur.

*

The thing about Arthur was they had put him to work.

It was in the power station, just as Amy had said, and Arthur didn't like it. The fact that he didn't like it was a splendid reason for staying away from there, but I let my kind heart overrule my good sense and paid him a visit.

It was way over on the East Side, miles and miles from any civilized area. I borrowed Amy's MG, and borrowed Amy to go with it, and the two of us packed a picnic lunch and set out. There were reports of deer on Avenue A, so I brought a rifle, but we never saw one; and if you want my opinion, those reports were nothing but wishful thinking. I mean if people couldn't survive, how could deer?

We finally threaded our way through the clogged streets and parked in front of the power station.

"There's supposed to be a guard," Amy said doubtfully.

I looked. I looked pretty carefully, because if there was a guard, I wanted to see him. The Major's orders were that vital defense installations—such as the power station, the PX and his own barracks building—were to be guarded against trespassers on a shoot-on-sight basis and I wanted to make sure that the guard knew we were privileged persons, with passes signed by the Major's own hand. But we couldn't find him. So we walked in through the big door, peered around, listened for the sounds of machinery and walked in that direction.

And then we found him; he was sound asleep. Amy, looking indignant, shook him awake.

"Is that how you guard military property?" she scolded. "Don't you know the penalty for sleeping at your post?"

The guard said something irritable and unhappy. I got her off his back with some difficulty, and we located Arthur.

Picture a shiny four-gallon tomato can, with the label stripped off, hanging by wire from the flashing-light panels of an electric computer. That was Arthur. The shiny metal cylinder was his prosthetic tank; the wires were the leads that served him for fingers, ears and mouth; the glittering panel was the control center for the Consolidated Edison Eastside Power Plant No. 1.

"Hi, Arthur," I said, and a sudden ear-splitting thunderous hiss was his way of telling me that he knew I was there.

I didn't know exactly what it was he was trying to say and I didn't want to; fortune spares me few painful moments, and I accept with gratitude the ones it does. The Major's boys hadn't bothered to bring Arthur's typewriter along—I mean who cares what a generator-governor had to offer in the way of conversation?—so all he could do was blow off steam from the distant boilers.

*

Well, not quite all. Light flashed; a bucket conveyor began crashingly to dump loads of coal; and an alarm gong began to pound.

"Please, Arthur," I begged. "Shut up a minute and listen, will you?"

More lights. The gong rapped half a dozen times sharply, and stopped.

I said: "Arthur, you've got to trust Vern and me. We have this thing figured out now. We've got the *Queen Elizabeth*—"

A shattering hiss of steam—meaning delight this time, I thought. Or anyway hoped.

"—and its only a question of time until we can carry out the plan. Vern says to apologize for not looking in on you—" *hiss*—"but he's been busy. And after all, you know it's more important to get everything ready so you can get out of this place, right?"

"Psst," said Amy.

She nodded briefly past my shoulder. I looked, and there was the guard, looking sleepy and surly and definitely suspicious.

I said heartily: "So as soon as I fix it up with the Major, we'll arrange for something better for you. Meanwhile, Arthur, you're doing a capital job and I want you to know that all of us loyal New York citizens and public servants deeply appreciate—"

Thundering crashes, bangs, gongs, hisses, and the scream of a steam whistle he'd found somewhere.

Arthur was mad.

"So long, Arthur," I said, and we got out of there—just barely in time. At the door, we found that Arthur had reversed the coal scoops and a growing mound of it was pouring into the street where we'd left the MG parked. We got the car started just as the heap was beginning to reach the bumpers, and at that the paint would never again be the same.

Oh, yes, he was mad. I could only hope that in the long run he would forgive us, since we were acting for his best interests, after all.

Anyway, I *thought* we were.

*

Still, things worked out pretty well—especially between Amy and me. Engdahl had the theory that she had been dodging the Major so long that *anybody* looked good to her, which was hardly flattering. But she and I were getting along right well.

She said worriedly: "The only thing, Sam, is that, frankly, the Major has just about made up his mind that he wants to marry me—"

"He *is* married!" I yelped.

"Naturally he's married. He's married to—so far—one hundred and nine women. He's been hitting off a marriage a month for a good many years now and, to tell you the truth, I think he's got the habit Anyway, he's got his eye on me."

I demanded jealously: "Has he said anything?"

She picked a sheet of onionskin paper out of her bag and handed it to me. It was marked *Top Secret*, and it really was, because it hadn't gone through his regular office—I knew that because I was his regular office. It was only two lines of text and sloppily typed at that:

Lt. Amy Bankhead will report to HQ at 1700 hours 1 July to carry out orders of the Commanding Officer.

The first of July was only a week away. I handed the orders back to her.

"And the orders of the Commanding Officer will be—" I wanted to know.

She nodded. "You guessed it."

I said: "We'll have to work fast."

*

On the thirtieth of June, we invited the Major to come aboard his palatial new yacht.

"Ah, thank you," he said gratefully. "A surprise? For my birthday? Ah, you loyal members of my command make up for all that I've lost—all of it!" He nearly wept.

I said: "Sir, the pleasure is all ours," and backed out of his presence. What's more, I meant every word.

It was a select party of slightly over a hundred. All of the wives were there, barring twenty or thirty who were in disfavor—still, that left over eighty. The Major brought half a dozen of his favorite officers. His bodyguard and our crew added up to a total of thirty men.

We were set up to feed a hundred and fifty, and to provide liquor for twice that many, so it looked like a nice friendly brawl. I mean we had our radio operator handing out highballs as the guests stepped on board. The Major was touched and delighted; it was exactly the kind of party he liked.

He came up the gangplank with his face one great beaming smile. "Eat! Drink!" he cried. "Ah, and be merry!" He stretched out his hands to Amy, standing by behind the radio op. "For tomorrow we wed," he added, and sentimentally kissed his proposed bride.

I cleared my throat. "How about inspecting the ship, Major?" I interrupted.

"Plenty of time for that, my boy," he said. "Plenty of time for that." But he let go of Amy and looked around him. Well, it was worth looking at. Those Englishmen really knew how to build a luxury liner. God rest them.

The girls began roaming around.

It was a hot day and late afternoon, and the girls began discarding jackets and boleros, and that began to annoy the Major.

"Ah, cover up there!" he ordered one of his wives. "You too there, what's-your-name. Put that blouse back on!"

It gave him something to think about. He was a very jealous man, Amy had said, and when you stop to think about it, a jealous man with a hundred and nine wives to be jealous of really has a job. Anyway, he was busy watching his wives and keeping his military cabinet and his bodyguard busy too, and that made him too busy to notice when I tipped the high sign to Vern and took off.

VI

In Consolidated Edison's big power plant, the guard was friendly. "I hear the Major's over on your boat, pal. Big doings. Got a lot of the girls there, hey?"

He bent, sniggering, to look at my pass.

"That's right, pal," I said, and slugged him.

Arthur screamed at me with a shrill blast of steam as I came in. But only once. I wasn't there for conversation. I began ripping apart his comfy little home of steel braces and copper wires, and it didn't take much more than a minute before I had him free. And that was very fortunate because, although I had tied up the guard, I hadn't done it very well, and it was just about the time I had Arthur's steel case tucked under my arm that I heard a yelling and bellowing from down the stairs.

The guard had got free.

"Keep calm, Arthur!" I ordered sharply. "We'll get out of this, don't you worry!"

But he wasn't worried, or anyway didn't show it, since he couldn't. I was the one who was worried. I was up on the second floor of the plant, in the control center, with only one stairway going down that I knew about, and that one thoroughly guarded by a man with a grudge against me. Me, I had Arthur, and no weapon, and I hadn't a doubt in the world that there were other guards around and that my friend would have them after me before long.

Problem. I took a deep breath and swallowed and considered jumping out the window. But it wasn't far enough to the ground.

Feet pounded up the stairs, more than two of them. With Arthur dragging me down on one side, I hurried, fast as I could, along the steel galleries that surrounded the biggest boiler. It was a nice choice of alternatives—if I stayed quiet, they would find me; if I ran, they would hear me, and then find me.

But ahead there was—what? Something. A flight of stairs, it looked like, going out and, yes, *up*. Up? But I was already on the second floor.

"Hey, you!" somebody bellowed from behind me.

I didn't stop to consider. I ran. It wasn't steps, not exactly; it was a chain of coal scoops on a long derrick arm, a moving bucket arrangement for unloading fuel from barges. It did go up, though, and more important it went *out*. The bucket arm was stretched across the clogged roadway below to a loading tower that hung over the water.

If I could get there, I might be able to get down. If I could get down—yes, I could see it; there were three or four mahogany motor launches tied to the foot of the tower.

And nobody around.

I looked over my shoulder, and didn't like what I saw, and scuttled up that chain of enormous buckets like a roach on a washboard, one hand for me and one hand for Arthur.

*

Thank heaven, I had a good lead on my pursuers—I needed it. I was on the bucket chain while they were still almost a city block behind me, along the galleries. I was halfway across the roadway, afraid to look down, before they reached the butt end of the chain.

Clash-clatter. *Clank!* The bucket under me jerked and clattered and nearly threw me into the street. One of those jokers had turned on the conveyor! It was a good trick, all right, but not quite in time. I made a flying jump and I was on the tower.

I didn't stop to thumb my nose at them, but I thought of it.

I was down those steel steps, breathing like a spouting whale, in a minute flat, and jumping out across the concrete, coal-smeared yard toward the moored launches. Quickly enough, I guess, but with nothing at all to spare, because although I hadn't seen anyone there, there was a guard.

He popped out of a doorway, blinking foolishly; and overhead the guards at the conveyor belt were screaming at him. It took him a second to figure out what was going on, and by that time I was in a launch, cast off the rope, kicked it free, and fumbled for the starting button.

It took me several seconds to realize that a rope was required, that in fact there was no button; and by then I was floating yards away, but the pudgy pop-eyed guard was also in a launch, and he didn't have to fumble. He knew. He got his motor started a fraction of a second before me, and there he was, coming at me, set to ram. Or so it looked.

I wrenched at the wheel and brought the boat hard over; but he swerved too, at the last moment, and brought up something that looked a little like a spear and a little like a sickle and turned out to be a boathook. I ducked, just in time. It sizzled over my head as he swung and crashed against the windshield. Hunks of safety glass splashed out over the forward deck, but better that than my head.

Boathooks, hey? I had a boathook too! If he didn't have another weapon, I was perfectly willing to play; I'd been sitting and taking it long enough and I was very much attracted by the idea of fighting back. The guard recovered his balance, swore at me, fought the wheel around and came back.

We both curved out toward the center of the East River in intersecting arcs. We closed. He swung first. I ducked—

And from a crouch, while he was off balance, I caught him in the shoulder with the hook.

He made a mighty splash.

I throttled down the motor long enough to see that he was still conscious.

"*Touché*, buster," I said, and set course for the return trip down around the foot of Manhattan, back toward the *Queen*.

*

It took a while, but that was all right; it gave everybody a nice long time to get plastered. I sneaked aboard, carrying Arthur, and turned him over to Vern. Then I rejoined the Major. He was making an inspection tour of the ship—what he called an inspection, after his fashion.

He peered into the engine rooms and said: "Ah, fine."

He stared at the generators that were turning over and nodded when I explained we needed them for power for lights and everything and said: "Ah, of course."

He opened a couple of stateroom doors at random and said: "Ah, nice."

And he went up on the flying bridge with me and such of his officers as still could walk and said: "Ah."

Then he said in a totally different tone: "What the devil's the matter over there?"

He was staring east through the muggy haze. I saw right away what it was that was bothering him—easy, because I knew where to look. The power plant way over on the East Side was billowing smoke.

"Where's Vern Engdahl? That gadget of his isn't working right!"

"You mean Arthur?"

"I mean that brain in a bottle. It's Engdahl's responsibility, you know!"

Vern came up out of the wheelhouse and cleared his throat. "Major," he said earnestly, "I think there's some trouble over there. Maybe you ought to go look for yourself."

"Trouble?"

"I, uh, hear there've been power failures," Vern said lamely. "Don't you think you ought to inspect it? I mean just in case there's something serious?"

The Major stared at him frostily, and then his mood changed. He took a drink from the glass in his hand, quickly finishing it off.

"Ah," he said, "hell with it. Why spoil a good party? If there are going to be power failures, why, let them be. That's my motto!"

Vern and I looked at each other. He shrugged slightly, meaning, well, we tried. And I shrugged slightly, meaning, what did you expect? And then he glanced upward, meaning, take a look at what's there.

But I didn't really have to look because I heard what it was. In fact, I'd been hearing it for some time. It was the Major's entire air force—two helicopters, swirling around us at an average altitude of a hundred feet or so. They showed up bright against the gathering clouds overhead, and I looked at them with considerable interest—partly because I considered it an even-money bet that one of them would be playing crumple-fender with our stacks, partly because I had an idea that they were not there solely for show.

I said to the Major: "Chief, aren't they coming a little close? I mean it's *your* ship and all, but what if one of them takes a spill into the bridge while you're here?"

He grinned. "They know better," he bragged. "Ah, besides, I want them close. I mean if anything went wrong."

I said, in a tone that showed as much deep hurt as I could manage: "Sir, what could go wrong?"

"Oh, you know." He patted my shoulder limply. "Ah, no offense?" he asked.

I shook my head. "Well," I said, "let's go below."

*

All of it was done carefully, carefully as could be. The only thing was, we forgot about the typewriters. We got everybody, or as near as we could, into the Grand Salon where the food was, and right there on a table at the end of the hall was one of the typewriters clacking away. Vern had rigged them up with rolls of paper instead of sheets, and maybe that was ingenious, but it was also a headache just then. Because the typewriter was banging out:

LEFT FOUR THIRTEEN FOURTEEN AND TWENTYONE
BOILERS WITH A FULL HEAD OF STEAM AND THE SAFETY
VALVES LOCKED BOY I TELL YOU WHEN THOSE THINGS
LET GO YOURE GOING TO HEAR A NOISE THATLL KNOCK
YOUR HAT OFF

The Major inquired politely: "Something to do with the ship?"

"Oh, *that*," said Vern. "Yeah. Just a little, uh, something to do with
the ship. Say, Major, here's the bar. Real scotch, see? Look at the
label!"

The Major glanced at him with faint contempt—well, he'd had the
pick of the greatest collection of high-priced liquor stores in the
world for ten years, so no wonder. But he allowed Vern to press a
drink on him.

And the typewriter kept rattling:

LOOKS LIKE RAIN ANY MINUTE NOW HOO BOY IM GLAD
I WONT BE IN THOSE WHIRLYBIRDS WHEN THE STORM
STARTS SAY VERN WHY DONT YOU EVER ANSWER ME Q
Q ISNT IT ABOUT TIME TO TAKE OFF XXX I MEAN GET
UNDER WEIGH Q Q

Some of the "clerks, typists, domestic personnel and others"—that
was the way they were listed on the T/O; it was only coincidence
that the Major had married them all—were staring at the typewriter.

"Drinks!" Vern called nervously. "Come on, girls! Drinks!"

*

The Major poured himself a stiff shot and asked: "What *is* that
thing? A teletype or something?"

"That's right," Vern said, trailing after him as the Major wandered
over to inspect it.

I GIVE THOSE BOILERS ABOUT TEN MORE MINUTES SAM
WELL WHAT ABOUT IT Q Q READY TO SHOVE OFF Q Q

The Major said, frowning faintly: "Ah, that reminds me of
something. Now what is it?"

"More scotch?" Vern cried. "Major, a little more scotch?"

The Major ignored him, scowling. One of the "clerks, typists" said:
"Honey, you know what it is? It's like that pross you had, remember?
It was on our wedding night, and you'd just got it, and you kept
asking it to tell you limericks."

The Major snapped his fingers. "Knew I'd get it," he glowed. Then abruptly he scowled again and turned to face Vern and me. "Say—" he began.

I said weakly: "The boilers."

The Major stared at me, then glanced out the window. "What boilers?" he demanded. "It's just a thunderstorm. Been building up all day. Now what about this? Is that thing—"

But Vern was paying him no attention. "Thunderstorm?" he yelled. "Arthur, you listening? Are the helicopters gone?"

YESYESYES

"Then shove off, Arthur! Shove off!"

The typewriter rattled and slammed madly.

The Major yelled angrily: "Now listen to me, you! I'm asking you a question!"

But we didn't have to answer, because there was a thrumming and a throbbing underfoot, and then one of the "clerks, typists" screamed: "The dock!" She pointed at a porthole. "It's moving!"

*

Well, we got out of there—barely in time. And then it was up to Arthur. We had the whole ship to roam around in and there were plenty of places to hide. They had the whole ship to search. And Arthur was the whole ship.

Because it was Arthur, all right, brought in and hooked up by Vern, attained to his greatest dream and ambition. He was skipper of a superliner, and more than any skipper had ever been—the ship was his body, as the prosthetic tank had never been; the keel his belly, the screws his feet, the engines his heart and lungs, and every moving part that could be hooked into central control his many, many hands.

Search for us? They were lucky they could move at all! Fire Control washed them with salt water hoses, directed by Arthur's brain. Watertight doors, proof against sinking, locked them away from us at Arthur's whim.

The big bull whistle overhead brayed like a clamoring Gabriel, and the ship's bells tinkled and clanged. Arthur backed that enormous ship out of its berth like a racing scull on the Schuylkill. The four giant screws lashed the water into white foam, and then the thin mud they sucked up into tan; and the ship backed, swerved, lashed the water, stopped, and staggered crazily forward.

Arthur brayed at the Statue of Liberty, tooted good-by to Staten Island, feinted a charge at Sandy Hook and really laid back his ears and raced once he got to deep water past the moored lightship.

We were off!

Well, from there on, it was easy. We let Arthur have his fun with the Major and the bodyguards—and by the sodden, whimpering shape they were in when they came out, it must really have been fun for him. There were just the three of us and only Vern and I had guns—but Arthur had the *Queen Elizabeth*, and that put the odds on our side.

We gave the Major a choice: row back to Coney Island—we offered him a boat, free of charge—or come along with us as cabin boy. He cast one dim-eyed look at the hundred and nine "clerks, typists" and at Amy, who would never be the hundred and tenth.

And then he shrugged and, game loser, said: "Ah, why not? I'll come along."

*

And why not, when you come to think of it? I mean ruling a city is nice and all that, but a sea voyage is a refreshing change. And while a hundred and nine to one is a respectable female-male ratio, still it must be wearing; and eighty to thirty isn't so bad, either. At least, I guess that was what was in the Major's mind. I know it was what was in mine.

And I discovered that it was in Amy's, for the first thing she did was to march me over to the typewriter and say: "You've had it, Sam. We'll dispose with the wedding march—just get your friend Arthur here to marry us."

"Arthur?"

"The captain," she said. "We're on the high seas and he's empowered to perform marriages."

Vern looked at me and shrugged, meaning, you asked for this one, boy. And I looked at him and shrugged, meaning, it could be worse.

And indeed it could. We'd got our ship; we'd got our ship's company—because, naturally, there wasn't any use stealing a big ship for just a couple of us. We'd had to manage to get a sizable colony aboard. That was the whole idea.

The world, in fact, was ours. It could have been very much worse indeed, even though Arthur was laughing so hard as he performed the ceremony that he jammed up all his keys.

www.ingramcontent.com/pod-product-compliance
Lightning Source LLC
Chambersburg PA
CBHW050916120626
46552CB00004B/1598